THE YEAR OF
THE PERFECT CHRISTMAS TREE

An Appalachian Story
by **GLORIA HOUSTON**
pictures by **BARBARA COONEY**

Dial Books for Young Readers / New York

The following persons and institutions offered aid in our research
to make both the text and the illustrations authentic representations of the
Appalachian Mountain culture during the time of the setting of this story:

The Appalachian Cultural Center, Appalachian State University, Boone, N.C.
The Rural Life Museum, Mars Hill College, Mars Hill, N.C.
The Tweetsie Railroad, Inc., Blowing Rock, N.C.
Grandfather Mountain, Inc., Linville, N.C.
Hugh Morton, photographer, Linville, N.C.
Rogers Whitener, syndicated columnist, "Folk Ways and Folk Speech,"
Appalachian State University, Boone, N.C.
Bill & "Miss Kay" Wilkins, cabin restoration, Plumtree, N.C.
J. Myron Houston, local historian, Spruce Pine, N.C.

Published by Dial Books for Young Readers
A Division of NAL Penguin Inc.
2 Park Avenue, New York, New York 10016
Published simultaneously in Canada
by Fitzhenry & Whiteside Limited, Toronto
Text copyright © 1988 by Gloria McLendon Houston
Pictures copyright © 1988 by Barbara Cooney
Design by Atha Tehon
Printed in U.S.A.
(a)

7 9 10 8 6

Library of Congress Cataloging in Publication Data
Houston, Gloria McLendon. The year of the perfect Christmas tree.
Summary: Since Papa has left the Appalachian area to go to war,
Ruthie and her mother wonder how they will fulfill his obligation of getting
the perfect Christmas tree to the town for the holiday celebration.
[1. Christmas trees—Fiction. 2. Christmas—Fiction.
3. Appalachian Region—Fiction. 4. World War, 1914-1918—United States—Fiction.]
I. Cooney, Barbara, 1917—   , ill. II. Title.
PZ7.H8184Ye 1988   [E]   87-24551
ISBN 0-8037-0299-X ISBN 0-8037-0300-7 (lib. bdg.)

The art for each picture was created with acrylic paints.
It was then scanner-separated and reproduced in full color.

For Mama, Ruth Greene Houston   G. H.

...and for J. Myron   B. C.

It was getting toward Christmas in the valley of Pine Grove. The wise folk said the old woman in the sky was picking her geese, for the Appalachian Mountains lay blanketed with snow. The road wound like white ribbons around the misty blue ridges, tracked by the runners of wagons, sleds, and sleighs. Occasionally an auty-mobile chugged its way through the silence. Across the ocean the Great War raged, but in the valley all was at peace.

It was getting on toward the Christmas Ruthie would never forget. The Christmas when the village almost did not have a Christmas tree. It happened this way. Ruthie told me so.

"Come, my pretty young'un," Papa had said one day early in the spring. "It is time to choose the Christmas tree for the village church."

"But, Papa, Christmas will not come for a long while," said Ruthie. "The sarvice trees are just now in bloom."

"We must choose a special tree and mark it for the coming year. It is the custom in our village," said Papa, "for one family to give to all the folk in the village and up every hill and holler a Christmas tree for Pine Grove Church. This year it is our turn.

"Some years a timbering man will give a fat round laurel from the northy coves, the kind the outlanders call rhododendron. Other years the holler folk may bring a cedar to spread its fragrance throughout the village church."

"What kind of tree shall we have, Papa?" said Ruthie.

"We shall have a balsam Christmas tree, my pretty young'un," said Papa. "The balsam grows up the rocky craigs where only a venturesome man may go. The balsam is a perfect tree. It grows up high, near to heaven."

So Papa and Ruthie rode on Old Piedy's back across the high cliffs and along the craigs looking for the perfect balsam Christmas tree. They rode and rode, from early morning until the sun was high in the sky.

Finally they saw it. Growing on the edge of a high cliff on Grandfather Mountain. Alone, with no other trees around it. Its green color was dark and rich. It was the perfect shape and size, its tip-tip-top pointing up to heaven.

"This will be our perfect Christmas tree," said Papa. "And as is the custom, the selfsame year you shall be the heavenly angel in the village Christmas play. It is fitting that you should mark the Christmas tree." Papa took the red ribbon from Ruthie's coal-black curls. He lifted her high in his strong arms.

"Tie this to the tip-tip-top," he said.

Then he kissed the dimple in each of Ruthie's cheeks.

The summer came, and Papa was called away to be a soldier. He went to fight in a war far across the sea.

That year the timber was not cut. So Mama had no money to buy coffee, sugar, or cloth for new dresses. Mama and Ruthie drank peppermint tea sweetened with honey. Mama lowered the hems of Ruthie's dresses and embroidered pretty flowers over the tears and mends. Together they tended the little garden, growing vegetables to eat.

And every night Mama tucked Ruthie into her little bed and listened as she said the same prayer.

"Please send my papa home for Christmas," Ruthie whispered. "And please have old St. Nicholas bring me a doll with a beautiful dress, the color of cream, all trimmed with ribbons and lace."

One day that fall, when the dried corn shocks rustled in the breeze, a package came from Papa. In it were soft silk stockings for Mama and blue satin hair ribbons for Ruthie. There was a letter too.

"I'll be home for Christmas," the letter said. "The war is finally over. The Armistice was signed today!"

The days passed. Each day Ruthie ran home from school as fast as the deer that fed by the stream.

"Is Papa home?" she called as she ran up the steps.

But every day Mama said, " Not today. Maybe tomorrow. He will come on the Tweetsie train."

The days passed. Ruthie listened for the squeaky whistle of the little train the mountain folk called Tweetsie, as it chugged through the valley and up the mountainside. One day Mama and Ruthie harnessed Old Piedy to the sled and went to the station at Pineola. But when the other men from the village stepped down from the train, Papa was not with them.

Soon there was only one more day until Christmas Eve. Over at the school Miss Jenny and her pupils were practicing the Christmas play.

The children sang the Appalachian lullaby "Jesus, Jesus, rest your head. You have got a manger bed."

Miss Jenny chose the boy and girl who would be Mary and Joseph. Then she called Ruthie's name.

"This year you shall be the heavenly angel," Miss Jenny said. "This is the year your papa will give the church its Christmas tree."

Miss Jenny helped Ruthie climb up to stand on the teacher's chair so it would look as if she were up in the sky. Miss Jenny showed her how to hold her arms just so.

"If you wear a dress with great big sleeves," said Miss Jenny, "it will look like you have wings."

"Mama, Mama," said Ruthie, as she ran up the front steps that day. "I must have a new dress with great big sleeves. I am going to be the heavenly angel when Papa gives the Christmas tree."

"Oh, my pretty young'un," said Mama. "I have no cloth to make a dress with great big sleeves. And I have no money until your papa comes home." Mama kissed the dimple in each of Ruthie's cheeks and hugged her daughter tightly.

That night the preacher from Pine Grove Church knocked at the door.

"Tomorrow is Christmas Eve, Miz Green," he said. "And Tom is not yet home from the war. Chad McKinney has been saving a prime cedar on his bottom land for Christmas next. He'd as leave cut the tree this year."

"This is the year our family gives the tree," said Mama. "Tom chose it before he went away to war."

"I had hoped you would heed my wish," said the preacher. "The church must have a Christmas tree when the morrow comes."

"Tom is as good as his word. Our family will give the tree this year," said Mama.

Late that night Mama wakened Ruthie. They dressed in their warm coats, hats, and mittens. Mama hitched Old Piedy to the big sled Papa used to haul fire logs down from the ridges. The moon shone silver as Mama and Ruthie made their way up the hill. Ruthie carried the lantern.

As they came to the dark woods the winter moon made strange shadows on the snow.

"Mama, I'm afraid," said Ruthie.

"No need to be afraid," said Mama. "We're off to get the perfect balsam Christmas tree."

Mama began to sing "I wonder as I wander out under the sky." Ruthie joined in the song. Soon she forgot to be afraid.

Mama and Ruthie led Old Piedy and the sled up the hills and across the ridges, but they could not find the perfect balsam.

"Papa says the balsam grows high on the rocky craigs up near heaven where only a venturesome man will go," said Ruthie.

"The rocky craig," said Mama. "We have a long climb ahead."

Slowly they led Old Piedy along the ridge to the highest craig on Grandfather Mountain. They could see the village sleeping in the valley far below. Finally at the edge of the highest cliff they saw the balsam standing alone.

"There it is, Mama," Ruthie cried. "See, there's my ribbon bow tied to the tip-tip-top." Ruthie ran up the rocky craig as Mama and Old Piedy followed.

The blade of Papa's ax shone in the moonlight as Mama lifted it high. *Thwack! Crack!* the sounds echoed through the rocks and hills.

Then Mama picked up the saw and said, "Take hold of the end, my pretty young'un. Pull as hard as ever you can."

Mama pulled. Ruthie pulled. Pull. Pull. Back and forth until the perfect balsam Christmas tree fell softly into the snow. Ruthie and Mama lifted the tree onto the sled and tied it there.

Then they made their way down the ridge.

"I saw three ships come sailing in, on Christmas Day in the morning," they sang.

Through the soft snow they led Old Piedy to the church. Together they lifted the perfect balsam Christmas tree from the sled and stood it in the corner near the belfry wall. Just as the sun was rising over Doe Hill, they hurried home.

Tucking Ruthie into her little bed, Mama whispered, "The folk shall have their Christmas tree, and you shall be the heavenly angel this year."

Ruthie fell fast asleep, but Mama sat long by the firelight sewing as fast as her nimble fingers could move.

First she cut the ribbons and lace from a wedding dress the color of cream. From it she fashioned a smaller dress with flowing sleeves.

Then she took a soft silk stocking, stuffed it with lamb's wool, and stroked it until it was smooth and round. She embroidered it with two blue eyes, little black curls, and made a dimple in each cheek. From the scraps of Ruthie's dress she made a tiny dress just like it, all trimmed with ribbons and lace. She dressed the stocking doll in the tiny dress.

The sun was high in the winter sky when a knock came at the door. "Good Christmas Eve, Preacher Ollis," Mama said. "Do come in and spell yourself."

"Did you hear the news about the Christmas tree?" the preacher said. "A wondrous balsam, from up the high craigs, was found on the belfry porch this morning."

"Do tell! Do tell! What a wonder," said Mama.

"And that's not all. It's being told hereabouts that folks who live up the holler heard the angels singing high up on the ridge late into the night. And they were singing Christmas songs," said Preacher Ollis.

Ruthie hid her face in Mama's patchwork quilt so the preacher would not hear her laugh.

Daylight was fading when Mama helped Ruthie into the prettiest dress Ruthie had ever seen. It was made of softest silk, the color of cream, all trimmed with ribbons and lace. It had long, flowing sleeves.

"If you hold your arms just so," said Mama, "it will look like you have wings."

At the church the ladies of the valley had decorated the perfect balsam Christmas tree. Reflections of the tiny red candles in their shiny holders fastened to the tips of the branches shone in the windows. Tied to the lower branches of the tree were presents wrapped in pretty paper. On the tip-tip-top was a tiny angel.

The sexton rang the bell. From up and down the River Road, and from all the hills and hollers, the folk were coming to celebrate the Christmas tree. A choir of children sat by the organ. The three kings waited outside the belfry door. Behind the bed-sheet curtains, Mama helped the little Mary put her doll to bed in the manger straw. Ruthie climbed up and stood on the preacher's big chair.

The ladies pushed the bed-sheet curtains back. Ruthie could see herself in the dark church windows. She was careful to hold her arms just so. In her beautiful dress it looked as if she had wings.

"Behold, I bring you good tidings of great joy," said Ruthie the heavenly angel.

When the program was over, Ruthie went to sit with Mama on the front pew. Mama held her close.

Then the three kings came walking down the aisle, carrying lard pails filled with the Christmas treat pokes. Each bag contained a soft peppermint stick, some chocolate drops, an orange, and some hazelnuts.

Behind the kings walked old St. Nicholas. He carried his toe sack goody bag with him.

Old St. Nick visited the A-Men corner first. He gave each of the deacons a lump of coal or a willow switch. The folk in the church laughed.

Then to all the children who had misbehaved old St. Nick gave a willow switch or a lump of coal as well. Ruthie had been good that year, so she got a treat poke instead.

At last it was time to call the names on the presents tied to the tree. Every child in the church received a present. Everyone, that is, except Ruthie. A tear slipped down into the dimple in her cheek.

Then one of the kings reached to the tip-tip-top of the perfect balsam Christmas tree. He lifted the tiny angel down.

"Why, Ruthie," said old St. Nick, "this tiny angel looks just like you."

And it did. The tiny angel was wearing a dress just like Ruthie's. It was made of softest silk, the color of cream. It was trimmed with ribbons and lace. The sleeves were long and flowing, and it looked as if she had wings. The angel's curls were as black as coal, and she had a dimple in each cheek.

Ruthie hugged the tiny angel and kissed its silky cheek, which felt just like the silk stockings Papa had sent to Mama.

The preacher said the benediction, and St. Nicholas wished to one and all a happy Christmas. Slowly the people began leaving the church. Mama and Ruthie walked out the belfry door. St. Nicholas was standing there. A man in an Army uniform stood beside him.

"And here is another present for you, Ruthie," said St. Nicholas.

But Ruthie was so busy looking at the tiny angel that she did not notice until strong arms picked her up.

"Let me look at you, my pretty young'un," said Papa's voice.

And he hugged Ruthie, Mama, and the tiny angel all at the same time.

The village folk gathered around the church steps.

Someone from the village began to sing "Silent night. Holy night. All is calm. All is bright."

The folk in the village joined in. But Papa, Mama, Ruthie, and the tiny angel hardly heard. They just hugged each other some more.

And since that time, every year for more than sixty years, a tiny angel has stood on top of a perfect balsam Christmas tree. She wears a dress of softest silk, the color of cream, all trimmed with ribbons and lace. The sleeves are long and flowing, and it looks as if she has wings. The angel has coal-black curls and a dimple in each cheek.

That's how it happened. The Christmas of the heavenly angel and the perfect balsam Christmas tree.

Grandma Ruthie told me so.

CHILDREN'S ROOM

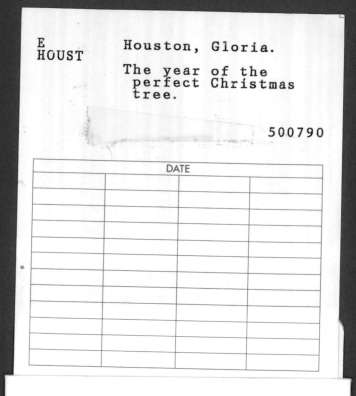